Christmas Day

Sam Grabiner's first play was *Boys on the Verge of Tears*. *Christmas Day* is his second.

by the same author from Faber

BOYS ON THE VERGE OF TEARS

SAM GRABINER

Christmas Day

faber

First published in 2025
by Faber and Faber Limited
The Bindery, 51 Hatton Garden
London, EC1N 8HN

Typeset by Brighton Gray
Printed and bound in the UK by CPI Group (Ltd), Croydon CR0 4YY

All rights reserved
© Sam Grabiner, 2025

Sam Grabiner is hereby identified as author
of this work in accordance with Section 77 of the
Copyright, Designs and Patents Act 1988

All rights whatsoever in this work, amateur or professional,
are strictly reserved. Applications for permission for any use
whatsoever including performance rights must be made in
advance, prior to any such proposed use,
to Independent Talent Group Limited,
40 Whitfield Street London, W1T 2RH

No performance may be given unless a licence
has first been obtained

A CIP record for this book
is available from the British Library

ISBN 978-0-571-40074-4

Printed and bound in the UK on FSC® certified paper in line with our continuing
commitment to ethical business practices, sustainability and the environment.
For further information see faber.co.uk/environmental-policy

Our authorised representative in the EU for product safety is
Easy Access System Europe, Mustamäe tee 50, 10621 Tallinn, Estonia
gpsr.requests@easproject.com

2 4 6 8 10 9 7 5 3 1

Christmas Day was first performed at the Almeida Theatre, London, on 9 December 2025, with the following cast:

Wren/Sphinx/Felix Jamie Ankrah
Noah Samuel Blenkin
Gabz Jessica Brindle
Maud Callie Cooke
Aaron Jacob Fortune-Lloyd
Elliot Nigel Lindsay
Tamara Bel Powley

Director James Macdonald
Set Designer Miriam Buether
Costume Designer Evie Gurney
Lighting Designer Jon Clark
Sound Designer Max Pappenheim
Intimacy Director Lucy Hind
Casting Director Amy Ball CDG
Costume Supervisor Sabia Smith
Props Supervisor Mary Halliday
Voice Coach Emma Woodvine
Assistant Director Sophia Golan

For Zamzam

Characters

Elliot
sixties

Noah
late twenties

Maud
late twenties

Tamara
late twenties

Wren
late twenties

Aaron
late twenties

Sphinx
mid-twenties

Felix
forties

Gabz
early thirties

CHRISTMAS DAY

What have I in common with the Jews? I have hardly anything in common with myself.

Franz Kafka

I feel at home in the entire world, wherever there are clouds and birds and human tears.

Rosa Luxemburg

Notes

The characters Wren, Sphinx and Felix are played by the same actor.

Elliot, Tamara, Aaron and Noah are people who talk over each other.

A forward-slash (/) signifies the point of interruption by the next speaker.

Words in square brackets are thought and not said.

I

A vast space.
Which was once an office, and is now lived in.
Dropped ceilings. Fire exit signs. Too many plug sockets.
There is something incoherent about the room, which has lived many lives and has thus taken on an impractical kind of madness. The recent domestic touches look ridiculous in their context.
From the whole, we get an impression of danger: wires, suspicious carpet stains, an industrial heater hanging from the ceiling. There is no loving landlord here.
Somewhere, a table with mismatched chairs.
The only light comes from a Christmas tree, which throws a strange glow,
And illuminates Elliot,
Who stares back at it.

Elliot Jesus fucking Christ.
Strange things aren't they.
I think they're strange.
They're sort of –
perverted?
I don't quite know what I mean but I think there's something perverted about a Christmas tree I think they're weird they've got an aura like a malicious kind of an aura it looks perverted and it gives me the creeps.

He turns away from the tree, looks around the room.

Are you –

Back to the tree.

Why have you even got one it's not natural to have a thing like that inside and besides it's seedy it makes the place feel like a place you'd do bad things like sell drugs or fuck a stranger or . . . eat heroin? Is that a thing people do eat . . .

It's weird in here I mean it's fucking weird you do know that?

I'd like to talk to you Noah I'd like to talk to you and your sister.

He takes a deep breath. In and out.

This old sage he's a sort of a

You know like a Hassidic kind of sage like a rabbi but –

I don't think people do eat heroin I know they inject it I'm not an idiot but they could and I'm sure they have if you can think of it then someone's done it and I guess it's just another way of getting it in there isn't it anyway this sage.

He's in Russia maybe or somewhere like that somewhere where there are Cossacks you know someone who's going to come in and –

He's a famous sage.

He's the kind of person that people travel miles to visit to be healed or to ask advice or to fast with you know how they're always

And recently he has been preaching a certain kind of very powerful mysticism.

A spiritual fervour has taken root and people have started to talk about the messiah about the coming of the Mashiach about the power of this rabbi and his teaching and how he has been laying the ground for the redemption of the world and the end of days –

Suddenly, the industrial gas heater bursts into life.

FUCKING hell.

Noah (*from off*) It does that.

Elliot looks around the place.

Elliot So you . . . you actually live here? Like –

It's a fucking office building Noah I mean COME ON what are you –

He takes a deep breath.

If your grandfather had seen this tree he would have cut off your cock.

(*The tree.*) Is it . . . alive?

Anyway some people are even saying that this man is the messiah himself and so the Cossacks or the authority you know whoever, the Egyptians, they arrest him they capture him because they see this powerful Jew as a kind of danger you know a sort of lynchpin someone who could start a rebellion who holds a lot of –

Jesus that fucking heater it looks like a bomb it doesn't look safe can you turn it off it's not even –

The heater turns off.
Elliot looks at it, suspicious, surprised.

This rabbi is a threat to the governing order and so they throw him in prison to rot and he sits in a cell in fucking Kiev or Vilnius or Warsaw or wherever and he is an enlightened man you know so he sort of meditates.

He prays.

He contemplates the Almighty.

And he is watched over by a guard. And this guard comes up to him and he starts to taunt him through the bars he says

(*To Noah in the other room.*) Listen to this

He says here's a question for you. If your God is so clever, then explain me this. When Adam and Eve are in the garden of Eden and they eat from the tree and God comes down and says in his booming voice:

Where art thou, Adam?

Well. If your God is all-powerful, if this God of yours is so special, all-knowing you know all-seeing, then why the fuck is he having to ask Adam where he is? He'd know already, wouldn't he?

And the Cossack, leaning up against the bars sort of smug sort of happy with himself, grins at the rabbi and says: Well? Riddle me that Jew-boy.

The rabbi meanwhile has been listening very carefully through all this.

And he stirs, and a gentle smile spreads across his lips and he looks up at the guard and he leans forward and he places one hand across his heart (*Elliot does so*) and with the other he reaches out towards the man (*he does so*) and he inhales (*he does*) preparing to speak –

When,
  As if from nowhere –
  Noah appears.

Noah What are you talking about?

And Elliot jumps out of his skin.

Elliot JESUS FUCK

Noah Sorry I / didn't

Elliot What the fuck

Noah Are you . . .
I mean I literally just walked in I

Elliot Why would you creep like that

Noah I didn't creep I

Elliot YOU CREPT

Noah Do you need –

Elliot FUCK

Noah I mean I really can't emphasise enough how I just –

Elliot Just give me a . . .

He catches his breath.

Noah Are you okay?

Elliot I'M FINE.

Noah Right. When someone shouts I'M FINE that aggressively it can be difficult to believe them. I mean you don't look fine. Terrible is maybe the word I'd use?

Do you need a doctor

Elliot Where did you even come / from

Noah I think it's something to do with the walls? With the way they split it up or something in the nineties or whatever you can't hear anything and then all of a sudden BANG there they are right there in the room next to you like an electric car or something

Elliot It's fine I'm just it's a family thing it's a shock thing it happens I'm just . . .

He has recovered now.

God what a –

And the industrial heater bursts into life again.

FUCKING CUNT

Noah Sorry that's sorry we really need to

Elliot What is that?

Noah Yeah it's the heater it's like I think it used to be a storage facility? And it had something in it they needed to keep warm like some kind of wood or tobacco or something and there's no central heating so I don't know Blade told us about it he's been here forever

Elliot Blade? What's Blade?

Noah No one nothing don't worry we managed to turn it off once but then it got too cold Blade's a person not a thing don't worry.

Elliot So this is your home?

Noah Yes this is my home what the hell is that supposed to mean

Elliot Are you squatting

Noah No we're not squatting

Elliot Do you need money? Because if you need money / I

Noah No Dad.

Elliot So this is a choice. To live here is a choice.

Noah Yes. Well. Sort of. It's a guardianship? Well it was a guardianship now you're actually kind of just a normal tenant it's sort of like a –

Elliot And it's cheap?

Noah Not really no / it's

Elliot Where's your sister

Noah Upstairs she'll / be

Elliot How many of you live here?

Noah Twelve at the moment

Elliot TWELVE?

Noah But they've all gone home for Christmas we've got it to ourselves today

Elliot Is this a commune?

Noah No Dad it is not a commune

Elliot Why do you live with twelve people

Noah I just do

Elliot That's too many people that's . . . ten too many people to live with.
   Jesus.

The heater turns off.

Noah's fucking Ark in here.

Noah starts laying the table. Elliot watches him.

Oi.

Noah looks at him.

Elliot Noah's fucking Ark in here. Just a joke.
Gis a smile boychik.

He does. It's hard won.

There he is. My boy.
So you're doing what, a dinner? Is this a Christmas dinner you're doing?

Noah No.
I mean I don't know I guess. It's Tamara's thing it's –
Jack's coming? He's visiting so yeah Jack's coming.

Elliot Jack? As in Jack Jack?

Noah Yes, as in Jack Jack. Well actually Aaron Jack. He goes by Aaron now.

Elliot Right.
And is that like a
Like a gender thing?

Noah Excuse me?

Elliot You know. Is that pronouns.

Noah No Dad. Aaron is his middle name, and he's using that as his first name now.

Elliot Sounds like a pronouns thing to me

Noah It's not a pronouns thing.
Do you know what a –
Sorry I don't understand how you could think that him using the name Aaron is about pronouns

Elliot Just trust me, it's a pronouns thing.

Noah gives up.

And she's okay with that? With him coming round?

Noah I dunno I think they're trying like a friends thing now

Elliot Mmm. He broke her last time. Didn't he?

Noah And it wasn't me by the way who got the tree that was someone else they get one every year apparently.

Noah lays the table.

Elliot And how's this girlfriend then I'm going to meet her?

Noah She has a name.

Elliot Yes. Yes she does.

A moment.

Noah Mau/d

Elliot Maud that's right.
Maud. Funny name.
English.

Noah I think it's actually technically Welsh

Elliot Don't think I've ever met a Maud.
You said things were tricky that you two were –

Noah (*ending the conversation*) It's fine.

Elliot And she's not [Jewish] . . .

Noah No she's not.

Elliot And I'm fine with that by the way.
Shouldn't she be with her family today?

Noah Uh-huh

Elliot Strange area. Bizarre out there. Just me and a bunch of foxes.

He watches Noah lay the table for a little while.

So the prison guard has asked this question.

Noah Have you looked at the news today –

Elliot The guard has asked the rabbi this question about Adam and Eve you know why does God have to ask Adam where he is if he's an all-knowing all-powerful force?

And the rabbi looks to the guard and he says: Do you think that this story, this story of the garden of Eden do you think it's a story of sin?

Of course, says the guard, it is the story of the original sin, of the very first sin. And the rabbi looks at him dead in the eye and he says: No. There is where you are wrong. This is not a story of sin. This, my friend, is a story of salvation.

Maud appears.

Maud Hello.

Noah jumps.

Noah JESUS FUCKING / FUCK

Maud WOW can you –

Noah Sorry I

Maud What's wrong with you

Noah Nothing's wrong with me I –

Elliot You crept

Maud I didn't creep I –

Noah My heart

Elliot You crept

Maud I just –

Elliot He's fine, he'll be fine

Noah It feels like it's about to blow up

Elliot It's not going to blow up

Noah How do you know

Elliot I just do.

I mean it does happen
Like it can happen
It's called cardiogenetic something cardiogenic shock something like that. You get a fright and then BANG that's it you just crumple but honestly, I think you'll be fine heart attacks do run in the family but not those type I don't think it's actually very common unless you specifically have some kind of underlying undiagnosed issue which I suppose is possible but I doubt / that

Noah STOP

Elliot Right yes sorry.

You'll be okay.
Trust me. It's just a family thing.
Your grandmother used to have it her way of dealing with it was to shout at your grandfather but I go for deep breaths these days. Hi. I'm Elliot. Nice to meet you.

Maud It's lovely to meet you I'm / Maud

Elliot You're Maud.

Maud Yes, that's right.

Elliot Welsh name is it?

Maud It's actually technically French but my mum thought it was Welsh.

A pause. Nobody really knows what to do.
Maud shakes herself all over and makes a strange sound.

Sorry.

Elliot You quite alright?

Maud Me?

Elliot Yes.

Maud Oh I'm fine. Sometimes you just have to . . .

Elliot Right.
   The place / is

Noah He thinks we're squatting

Elliot Maud you'll be interested in this. It's a story right about this old rabbi –

Maud You were talking about salvation

Elliot Yes that's right yes I was exactly

Noah Why would Maud be interested / in that

Maud I'm / interested

Elliot So the rabbi says to the guard: NO. It is not a story about sin it is a story about salvation.

Noah continues to lay the table. Maud helps.

You see as soon as God put man in a garden with a tree and said DON'T EAT FROM THAT TREE the outcome's obvious. They're human after all. The real moment of the story comes later. After the temptation after they have sinned when God comes down and says to his creation: Where have you gone?

Maud flicks a switch and a string of fairy lights light up the space.

At this point, Adam has a choice.

In the background we hear a faint rumble. It's a strange, unrecognisable sound.

He has to do a kind of . . . You know he has to . . . to confront himself in some way? He has to ask himself . . .

Maud and Noah ignore the sound, Elliot is distracted by it.

Where is your sister is she

The sound is growing and growing. Elliot looks around, starting to panic a little.

What the hell is –
　　Can you hear something?
　　Am I
　　Can you also

The rumble is now a roar. It grows and grows and feels like it is moving right through the space.

What THE FUCK is

Elliot puts his hands over his ears, crouches down on the floor and closes his eyes.
　　The rumble passes off in the distance.
　　And then, Tamara is standing there.

Tamara (*to Elliot*) What the fuck are you doing here

Elliot spins around and jumps out of his skin.

Elliot FUCKING HELL TAMARA!!!

And like a freight train herself:

Tamara Since when were you coming round did he tell you he was coming round? I didn't know you were coming round why are you on the floor what's the matter wait are you wearing a Christmas jumper is he wearing a Christmas jumper WHY are you wearing a Christmas jumper Jesus those trousers I can basically see your penis

Elliot What WAS that?

Tamara If I'd known you were coming I would have –
　　(*To Noah.*) You knew he was coming didn't you?
　　(*To Maud.*) Did you know he was coming

Maud Me?

Tamara You look like a nonce you look like Rolf Harris Jesus are you actually dressed up for Christmas right now?

Elliot No I'm dressed up for the fucking Chief Rabbi of course I'm dressed up for Christmas

Tamara Okay wow that was aggressive and uncalled for

Maud Was Rolf Harris a paed/ophile?

Tamara / Yes

Noah Yeah

Elliot I'm sorry / I

Maud Oh I'm thinking of Bill Oddie

Tamara Why are you on the floor? And since when do you just come around unannounced? Have you seen the news have you seen the images have you looked at / the news?

Noah Tamara don't

Maud Sorry Elliot we should / have mentioned

Tamara I live twenty minutes from you all my adult life and now all of a sudden we're getting unannounced house visits

Noah It's the train

Tamara Ohhhh / the

Maud Yeah the

Elliot What is this place

Noah It's the Northern / Line

Tamara It's the / Tube

Maud It happens

Elliot The what?

Noah The Tube runs underneath.

Tamara Why are those here

Noah I thought today they wouldn't be running / but

Maud It isn't supposed to run on Christmas Day

Tamara Hello am I invisible what are those?

Noah What do you mean what are those what do you think they are

Tamara This isn't a Christmas lunch

Noah I know it isn't a
They're fairy lights Tam calm down

Tamara Don't tell me to calm down

Elliot That's the Tube?! As in
The Tube. That. The Tube. That was the Tube? Like the London / Under—

Tamara STOP saying the word Tube.

A moment.

Noah Yes. It is.

Tamara It does have a psychotic kind of energy about it I agree.

Elliot That's completely fucking insane.

Silence. They all stand there, arriving here in the room together.
   The heater bursts into life.
   None of them react.
   The heater turns off.

Noah Food's on the way

Tamara Where did you / order

Noah Place on the roundabout.
We should finish laying the table.

Noah and Maud go back to laying the table. Tamara watches.

Maud You were telling us a story Elliot.

Nothing.

Noah Dad?

Elliot Huh?

Maud You were telling us a story. About Adam and Eve.

Elliot Yes, yes that's right.

So this rabbi says yeah he says right that's right yes the real moment of the Adam and Eve story is when God says to Adam, Where art thou? Because it's then, you see, it's then that Adam has a choice. He has done wrong, but he has an opportunity now to stand before God and say: Here I am. I have failed. And I will take responsibility. And you may do with me what you will. He stops hiding. From himself. From the Almighty. And that is where the story of the human begins. It's not a fall, it's a kind of ascension. And the rabbi looks up to the guard and he says: What's your name? And the guard replies: Janov. My name is Janov. And the rabbi says to the guard: And you, my friend, I ask you the same thing. Where art thou, Janov?

And the guard looks down at himself and he sees that he is a guard and that this rabbi is his prisoner and that he has before him a holy man a man of messianic power.

Anyway a few days later there's a gigantic pogrom and the rabbi is drowned his followers are dismembered the prison is burned and yeah every Jew within a hundred miles is slaughtered.

Anyway, I'm doing therapy.

Noah / What

Maud Wow –

Tamara Wait you're what –

Noah Therapy –

Tamara Since when –

Maud That's great –

Noah Like therapy, therapy?

Elliot But isn't that a fascinating story?

Tamara Since when I said

Elliot Like what's the moral you know it sort of makes you think it has a moral and then at the end / you just

Noah You mean like actual therapy?

Tamara Oh shut up Noah of course actual therapy

Noah Well it could be / like

Tamara It could be what?

Noah I don't know physiotherapy

Tamara It's not physiotherapy Dad is it physiotherapy

Elliot What? No, no. It's like talking you know

Tamara For how long

Elliot I don't know a few months now maybe

Noah Fucking hell

Tamara Dad that's / great

Noah A few months

Maud How exciting

Elliot Yes it's more than great it's actually . . .
 It's a bizarre story though isn't it, like to think of Adam and Eve not as like fuck ups like not as the original fuck ups but I do wonder what the moral is and then / when they

Tamara Wait wait what changed? And why didn't you tell me? Did you use that link I sent?

Elliot It's an American actually

Tamara An American

Noah Right

Elliot Yeah it's this American woman we do it on Zoom you know remarkable really

Noah Well that's good

Elliot It's a story you've heard your whole life and then it's like flipped upside down

Tamara I wish you had told me Dad I would have helped you find someone, you know in person is good too you should try in person does he does she do it in person

Elliot She's in New York / though so

Tamara Right well you know there are therapists who live in London too? Like. Loads. Too many.

Elliot It was all Sarah's idea

Tamara Excuse me?

Elliot She's been amazing and it's someone who she knows like a recommendation

Tamara I've been telling you to do therapy for ten years Dad

Noah Tammy

Tamara Don't Tammy me I've been working on this all my adult life then Sarah tells him to and all of a sudden he's telling us weird stories about rabbis and pogroms

Elliot It is a funny story though / isn't it

Tamara Is it someone who Sarah's seen before? Because if it is I think that's fucked. You shouldn't be seeing the same therapist as your girlfriend it needs to be your own space where you can express yourself freely a place where you can talk about Sarah
  I mean
  yeah
  I imagine in fact you actually have quite a lot to say about Sarah to your therapist I mean Jesus I know I do is

it a Jew? Is it a New York Jew? I bet it's some Upper West Side Jew she's got you with –

Elliot What's wrong with an Upper West Side / Jew

Tamara It sounds to me like your therapist is the exact same kind of person as your girlfriend

Noah Tamara.
   He's in therapy.
   That's great.

Tamara Sorry. Yeah. It's just. Yeah.
   You're right that's
   Sorry
   that's amazing Dad
   I
   I'm proud of you.

These last words push Elliot off an edge he didn't know he was on. He sobs.

Noah Oh my God.
   Are you

Tamara Dad oh no Dad I didn't mean to

Noah Wow.

They just stand there.

Maud How beautiful

Noah Tam are you . . .

*Tamara approaches Elliot,
   as if he were an unexploded bomb.*

Tamara Would you like a . . .

*She reaches out to put a hand on him
   When –
Wren, a man in nothing but shorts and a gaming headset, walks into the room from upstairs.*

They all watch him as he walks through the room towards the front door. He doesn't notice them.
We might or might not be able to tell that he is very stoned.
He's gone.

Elliot Did I hallucinate / that

Noah I thought he was with his family

Tamara What family

Elliot Who was that?

Maud That's Wren

Tamara I swear we had the place to / ourselves

Noah Do you think we need to invite him to dinner?

Elliot Sorry what's his name?

Tamara We are NOT eating with him

Maud He's called Wren

Elliot Right

Noah We should ask

Tamara Obviously we shouldn't ask remember last time with the –

Maud Yes of course the sriracha

Noah That was actually so weird

Tamara Isn't he at that gong bath in Devon –

Noah That's Dexter

Elliot Wren?
  Why?

Maud Why is he called Wren?

Elliot Yes

Maud You seem to be a man who is very interested in names, Elliot.

Wren comes back in. He is now holding a bag of takeaway food.
After a few steps, he sees them.

Wren Huh

        What I

Wow.

          You're huh

Maud Hi Wren

Wren Huh?

Maud Hi

He lifts his headphones off an ear.

Hello.

Wren Yeah. Wow.

Noah Merry Christmas

Wren What? Oh. Uh-huh yeah. Wow. Easy. It's all easy yeah.

Noah We put it on the group we're having a thing it's . . .

Wren I'm . . .
  Are you errr

        Yeah. Easy.

He leaves.

Elliot Seems like an affable chap.
Wren.
Like the architect.
Or the bird.

Maud I think they're the same.

*They stand there for a bit, not quite knowing what to do.
A train thunders through the space.
It's gone.*

Elliot I think I'm going to go to the is the . . .

Tamara The what

Elliot The toilet is it

Maud I can show you

Elliot That's okay I can / go

Noah It's complicated

Elliot Just tell me

Noah Come with me I'll show you it's actually genuinely complicated

Elliot It's the toilet Noah I can get to the toilet just tell / me

Tamara It's up the stairs out the door then round the corner

Noah Past the metal door on your left and then down the second of the two corridors the one with the green walls

Tamara Not the yellow walls

Maud Past the Henry the Eighth painting

Tamara But before the big evacuation chair thing in the glass case.

Noah Yeah there's a sign that says LOVELY BEANS on the door and you have to duck under this girder thing? You'll understand when you see it. That's the toilet.

Tamara The flush is kind of –

Noah You sort of wiggle it and then

Maud Up down up up down.

Elliot Right.
Are you in trouble with the police?

Tamara What?

Elliot Nothing, I . . .

Noah I'll show you

Elliot No I'd rather . . .

He's gone.
And like a coiled spring:

Tamara Oh my fucking God

Noah Fuck me
Did he cry? I don't think I've ever seen him cry

Tamara I've seen him cry

Noah When have you seen him cry?

Tamara Like when he thinks about Grandpa

Noah Yeah that / doesn't

Tamara When he talks about the holocaust

Noah Sure / but

Tamara Every time we land in Tel Aviv

Noah Felt weird

Tamara Fucking Sarah

Noah Thank God for Sarah

Tamara What do you MEAN thank God for Sarah?
(*An impression.*) Look hunny if you don't spend a little time focusing on yourself, then the people around you are not going to have their needs met.
What a fucking cunt.

Noah You know he's making kefir?

Tamara I literally cannot. The day he breaks up with her I will rejoice she has evil energy don't you think she has evil energy

Noah He's sending me mindfulness memes

Tamara Where do they even get the memes from I don't understand

Noah He told me yesterday that Esther Perel makes him proud to be Jewish

Tamara HA what the / actual

Noah He's sending me her TED Talks like ones about shagging and stuff

Tamara SHUT UP DON'T

Noah About pleasure? I think him and Sarah do ass stuff

Tamara What?

Noah Like, *his* ass I mean

Tamara NO! NO NOAH. STOP.

Noah Anyway we're almost at the six month mark she'll be gone soon enough

Tamara Please God.

The heater comes on.
 They all look at it.

Maud Do you think it's like, poisonous?

Like maybe it's the kind of thing that's actually toxic and in twenty years we'll all get this really specific kind of cancer and then they'll trace it back to that heater and we'll all be grouped in with Blade and Wren and Dexter and Gabz and the others and we'll like be together in eternity having randomly just lived in this place for like a year or whatever and it'll be because of this weird heater that we all just thought was normal you know like with that Russian film where they all just died of that thing.

The heater turns off.

Noah Shall we try and disable it or / whatever

Maud No, no. Just saying.

Tamara Has he texted?

Noah No

Tamara Have you seen the news have you seen what they've done

Noah Tamara / please

Tamara When will he be here?

Noah Any minute.

Tamara Do you think the table's okay

Noah It's fine

Tamara I'll light some candles maybe

Maud I like your hair Tamara.

Tamara It's so typical that he's making us wait for him

Noah He's come from across the world Tam

Tamara moves stuff around on the table. Noah watches her.

What about the quiz. Why don't we do a quiz?

Tamara I don't want to do a quiz

Noah Come on Tamara let's do it we've got this Christmas quiz thing

Tamara Jews don't quiz on Christmas

Noah What

Tamara This isn't Christmas.
It's very goyisher
To quiz

Noah What does that even mean
Come on let's do it. It's something Maud's family did it's nice come on.

Maud We don't need to do it

Noah I want to do it

Tamara I'm not doing it

Noah Some fairy lights and a quiz shouldn't be enough to topple your sense of self Tamara.
(*To Maud.*) Quiz master?

Tamara I'm not taking part

Noah Come on Maud

Maud Are you sure we really don't . . .

Noah Come on.

Maud takes her phone out to read.

Maud Alright. They're kind of random.
Who is taller Ant or Dec?

Tamara Oh my God that's so easy

Noah Oh yeah?

Tamara Come on

Noah You answer then

Tamara No I'm not doing it

Noah Is it Dec?

Tamara You are a moron

Noah How is anyone supposed to know that?

Tamara Obviously Ant isn't like an actual ant so he's taller

Maud Okay question two name every member of Girls Aloud

Tamara (*like a lightning bolt*) Nicola Roberts, Kimberley Walsh, Cheryl Cole, Nadine Coyle, Sarah Harding.

Maud Wow you. Wow.

Noah I thought you weren't involved in this

Tamara I'm not

Maud You really like Girls Aloud

Tamara That's two nil

Maud Who commanded the victory at the Battle of Waterloo?

Tamara Nelson?

Noah Napoleon?

Maud No.

Tamara Victoria

Noah OH FUCK it's I do actually know this fuck it's

Tamara Are they like a soldier

Maud I . . . I guess so?

Noah No shut up don't give her any clues / it's

Tamara Are they famous

Maud I guess it sort of depends on your like definition of / famous

Tamara Would we know them? Is it Cromwell it's Cromwell

Maud No

Tamara Nelson, it's Nelson

Maud Nope

Noah Yeah it's still not Nelson

Tamara William Pitt?

Noah FUCK FUCK it's I KNOW this

Tamara Are you sure it's not Nelson

Maud Positive yes

Noah FUCK

Tamara Because I'm pretty sure it's Nelson

Noah Come on Noah come on Noah think you fucking

Tamara Boudica?

Maud Erm I think she's like two thousand years too early maybe

Tamara Lord Byron

Maud Erm

Tamara Cecil Beaton?

Maud He's a 1950s fashion designer

Noah THE DUKE OF WELLINGTON!

Maud Correct!

Tamara FUCK YOU CUNT. Next.

Maud Erm

Tamara Come on come on come on

Maud What day of the week did the Queen die on?

Tamara What kind of a question is that

Maud I'm just reading / the

Noah Wednesday, it was Wednesday

Maud No

Noah Okay Tuesday

Maud You two are like yeah you're like really into quizzes aren't you

Noah Thursday?

Tamara What you're just going to name all the days of the week are you

Maud I'll take your first answer Noah. Tamara?

Tamara I don't care when the Queen died

Maud To go three one up

A moment.

Tamara Monday

Maud It was Thursday so that goes to Noah

Tamara What kind of bullshit rule is that

Noah I was closer

Tamara He was wrong

Noah I WAS CLOSER

Tamara NEXT

Maud What's the most northerly English county

Tamara We are North-West London Jews Maud we don't know / what

Noah Yorkshire?

Tamara It's Northumberland you fucking idiot

Maud Correct!

The harsh sound of a door buzzer.

Tamara Shit.

Noah Must be him.

Tamara Shit.

Noah I'll get it.

Noah leaves.
Tamara doesn't quite know what to do with herself.

Tamara Right shall we . . .
   Yeah nice.
   Do you want a drink?

Maud I'm fine thank you

Tamara Cool.

They stand there.

Maud Wow.

Tamara What?

Maud You really do look very beautiful Tamara, you've extraordinary eyes.

This comment almost makes Tamara cry.

Hey.
   Hey.
   None of that. Strength.

Tamara I'm gunna just one sec you know I'll yeah I'll

Tamara is gone.
   Maud stands there.
   We hear the sound of movement from off. Doors opening and closing.
   Maud closes her eyes and

Maud (*singing, to herself*)
   'In the bleak midwinter
   Frosty wind made moan
   Earth stood –'

Noah comes back in, carrying a suitcase.

Noah I'm gunna get Dad can you I think the food is out there the guy can't find the door but he's on like a bike it's sixty-seven that number you need to give

Maud I thought we were going to talk Noah –

33

Noah is gone.
 Maud goes up to the heater. Stares at it.
 She takes a step closer to it, looking it right in the eye. If it were to come on now, she'd burn her face. She takes a deep, deep breath.
 She leaves through the front door.
 The heater turns on.
 After some time, Aaron enters through the front door. He looks around the place. Taking it in.
 The heater turns off.
 Sphinx – a dishevelled man – enters from upstairs.

Sphinx My guy a very good afternoon to you.

I stayed with your friend last night.

Hit that vape when I woke up to be honest wow daddy kept me under for longer than anticipated.

It's strange isn't it? To be alone on a day like today. But it feeds the soul I do believe that. To be alone can be a source of great power.

Sphinx moves past a very confused-looking Aaron.

A very merry Christmas to you and your kin my brother.

Sphinx bows.
 And leaves.
 And then,
 Tamara enters.
 Shocked to find herself face-to-face and alone with Aaron, she freezes.
 They both stand there looking at one another.

Tamara Wow

Hi

Fucking

Hey-ho.

Found your way in alright. Funny you look yeah you look God you look . . .

How was the flight was it sorry wait where are your have you got a bag did you bring a suitcase because we can put it upstairs if you need that or a drink of water is that what people do when they get back from a journey

Bluh.

They look at each other.

Alright dickhead.

He smiles.

11

Maud, Noah, Elliot and Tamara are sat around the table, on which sits a mountain of takeaway Chinese food.
 They are transfixed by Aaron, who is mid-flow.
 He is a man who seems to glow. A great ease in his own skin.

Aaron The sun is coming up over the sea and there's this extraordinary quality to it. As if everything is in high definition. I suppose the light falls differently over there. I'm with my friends. There are seven of us. Ilana and Mayan and Yitzhak. I told you about Yitzhak didn't I Noh?

He nods.

It does feel like the rules are different, especially when it comes to friends. Friends seem easier to make? You're on a night out and it all just moves with this incredible ease. A kind of flow.
 So we're all together and we're sitting in this big heap and we're on this ledge just above the beach and we're smoking these cigs they've got with these short filters I actually brought some back for you they're absolutely fucking gorgeous you're gunna die, anyway, it's six in the morning maybe and we're lying there on the beach. A few joggers, a few people heading out early to work, a few other groups like us dotted around. And my friend stands up.
 And she starts walking towards the sea.
 Wordlessly.
 It's warm but it's not too warm, a real summer's morning, and we're all watching her as she walks out towards the ocean. She puts her cig in her mouth and she starts to take her clothes off, throwing a top off here and a shoe off

there and she's getting closer and closer to the sea. And she looks oughhh she looks . . . Otherworldly, really. We're all watching her but we're not talking we're just watching and she's walking naked now, smoking, her feet in the waves.

And the next thing I know we're all in there, we're all naked and we're swimming in this water that is like nothing I've ever seen let alone felt I didn't know water could be so . . .

We're swimming and laughing and I think some people are maybe fucking? And I look up at this morning sky and I take a deep breath and I dunk my head under the water and I come up again and it's like from that moment on, really it was like . . .

I don't know. It was as if something happened.

Anyway. It beats the comedown on the night bus through Finchley.

A moment.

Sorry. Tamara, you were saying.

A moment.

Maud Tamara?

Tamara / Huh?

Elliot You remember Eilat don't you? Those beaches in Eilat when we'd visit Grandma? What you're saying Jack reminds me very much of those beaches you two used to love / swimming

Tamara Aaron.

Elliot Excuse me?

Noah It's Aaron Dad, not Jack

Elliot Right yes of course Aaron, sorry Aaron

Aaron It takes some getting used to.
Eilat is beautiful.

Maud Tamara?

Tamara Yes. Okay. Well. Is everybody ready?
Good.
Before we eat this meal I thought it would be nice to –

Aaron (*singing*) MMMMMM DELICIOUS

Noah (*joining in*) /MMMMMM MMMMMM DELICIOUS

Aaron / MMMMMM MMMMMM DELICIOUS

Noah / MMMMMM DELICIOUS

Aaron MMMMMM DELICIOUS

Noah / MMMMMM MMMMMM DELICIOUS

Aaron MMMMMM MMMMMM DELICIOUS
TIME TO EAT SOME LOVELY FOOD

Noah TO PUT US IN A LOVELY MOOD

Aaron / MMMMMM DELICIOUS MMMM MMMM DELICIOUS

Noah MMMMMM DELICIOUS MMMM MMMM DELICIOUS

The boys are having fun.

(*Back in his normal voice.*) Sorry.

Tamara Done?

Noah Yes, yes.

Tamara Before we eat this food, I thought it'd be nice to say a few things

Aaron (*back to it*) IT'S LUNCH TIME

Noah BRUNCH TIME

Aaron MUNCH TIME

Noah CRUNCH TIME

Aaron / MMMMMMMMMMM DELICIOUS!

Noah MMMMMMMMMMM DELICIOUS!

Elliot (*the boys' song*) I don't remember this what is this –

Maud Tamara you were saying

Tamara I've been doing a lot of thinking recently.

Aaron Uh-huh, yeap.

Tamara This year. I mean this year it's been
Politically
And socially
And . . .
It's been
Well it's made me think. In new and different ways.
And so I thought it would be nice to say a few things before we start. Christmas Day is a strange time for us. And it's actually got like a fascinating history in the diaspora so I thought that before we start eating we could talk a little.
Noah

Noah What?

Tamara Historically, December twenty-fifth has been a dangerous day for us –

Elliot Dangerous?

Tamara You're living in some town in rural Lithuania in the 1890s and it's Christmas Day and the locals go to church or whatever and then they go back home and they eat their turkey or goose or you know and they drink and drink and then, when the sun has set, the mood might kick in for a little celebratory evening of Jew-bashing. Booze and the word of Christ are a historically bad mix. And so, Maud

Maud / huh

Tamara We tended to stay in our houses. Turn off the lights. Board up the doors.

And as the years went on and you know in Europe we're living in Europe in the nation whatever in the West –

Aaron Christendom. I think the word you are looking for is Christendom, Tamara

Tamara Don't take the piss

Aaron I'm not taking the piss

Noah You're taking the piss

Elliot What does that mean Christendom what does that word mean

Tamara It doesn't matter what it means what I'm saying is that this day has come to take on all sorts of different meanings for those of us who, in some way, sit outside of it

Maud Is this the Chinese food like you / were saying

Tamara So it's 1920 and you're a garment worker living on the Lower East Side

Aaron It is not 1920 and she is not a garment worker living on the Lower East Side

Tamara And the whole city closes down on Christmas Day. Where do you eat? What are the only restaurants open in your part of town

Aaron So Hymey and Rebecca sit down for some egg-fried rice

Tamara And it's become a tradition

Maud I think that's a very profound thing

Aaron You, Maud, have never had to watch an old Jew eat noodles –

Tamara I was reading about all this history you know all this crazy stuff about what it's been like being Jewish on this day what it *is* like and I was struck by something that I've been thinking about a lot recently about what this thing means you know? About all this history that we carry

Noah Wow

Tamara What?

Noah Nothing. I. Nothing.

Tamara Stop then

Noah Stop what

Tamara Breathing stop breathing like that

Noah You want me to stop / breathing?

Tamara This history keeps wanting to teach me the same lesson. Over and over. It is a history that puts us into a kind of relationship a kind of a complex relationship with all oppressed peoples. And this might not be a history that we are living today

Aaron That's not / true

Tamara Yes it is. It is a history that is in our bones though it is no longer in our lives, not like it was. And so I keep thinking that we have a kind of a decision to make. And a day like today reminds me of this decision, this choice we have, to build a kind of solidarity out of this history

Aaron A solidarity with who?

Tamara With all oppressed people all over the world

Aaron Big stuff Tam, big stuff

Tamara Yes. It is big / stuff

Aaron A lot of them don't like Jews

Tamara Oh my God Jack

Elliot What are all these words when did you learn all these words

Tamara Maud

Maud / Yes

Elliot I've always liked Christmas

Tamara I didn't say I didn't like / Christmas

Noah I'm so hungry

Elliot Is this what they mean when they say critical race theory?

Maud Well –

Elliot I didn't know we were involved in all that I thought that was just for shvartzers –

Tamara Dad!

Elliot What?

Noah That word

Tamara You can't –

Noah You shouldn't –

Elliot Oh come on

Maud What does that mean

Noah If someone called you a yid

Elliot That's different

Tamara Who has ever called anyone a yid

Elliot I've been / called

Tamara Maud

Maud Yes

Tamara Judaism is a religion of time, not of space.

Maud Right.

Noah What are / you

Tamara When the second temple was destroyed –

Aaron Here we fucking / go

Noah How long did it take us to bring up / the second temple

Elliot What do you know about the second temple

Tamara I actually know loads about the / second temple

Aaron I live there like I've been there I was there like two days / ago

Tamara MAUD.

Maud Hello.

Tamara Thousands of years ago there was a big temple in Jerusalem. And Judaism was what we might call a religion of space. There was a priesthood. And every year the most senior member of this priesthood journeyed into the most sacred inner chamber of this temple and in this sort of inner chamber bit, in the holy of holies, he saw God.

Noah Sort of

Tamara The Jewish people had a spatial conception of holiness. God was there. In that place. Sacrifices were made to him. And the land the land was sanctified the land was where it was you know it

Aaron And then it was destroyed

Tamara Yes and then the temple was destroyed

Noah By Romans

Aaron Sort of like Nazis in togas

Maud Yes I think / I know about this

Tamara And the surviving Jews were banished from the land and they set out for the first time into exile. Into the diaspora. And from here we see we see a sort of we see a transition into a Jewishness not of space, but of time.

What do you do if you have no temple? What do you do when you are a stranger in someone else's land?

Maud I don't / know

Tamara You keep the sabbath. You set aside a day that is untouchable. That's unlike any other day. It is time, now, that is holy, not space. And it is this practice that teaches us that on earth we shouldn't build. We should experience. Who needs a Pope and a Golden Temple?

Aaron (*quietly*) A nation state –

Tamara And it is this experience of exile that connects us to most people on this planet. Do you see? Do you see that?

Aaron There's another theory for why Jews went to Chinese restaurants on Christmas Day Maud and that's because you can order a dumpling and the pork is hidden inside so nobody can see / that you're eating it

Tamara What I'm trying to say is that I want to spend this day with the people I love. Experiencing what it is to live through time. And how overwhelmingly beautiful that is. And I want us to remember that that can happen anywhere. In fact it is an intrinsic part of who we are that that can happen anywhere. Where we are. That is where is holy. So. Merry December twenty-fifth.

The heater bursts into life.

L'Chaim.

They all l'chaim.

Noah Nice speech

Tamara throws daggers.

Seriously I . . . Seriously.

Aaron Right. Shall we?

Maud Crackers!

Noah Ooo yeah / crackers

Tamara Why did you have to / buy crackers

Noah Literally everybody loves crackers how can you not –

Elliot How do you do this do you

Noah I think you cross your hands

Aaron Really?

Noah Maud do you / cross

Maud You cross everyone crosses like this.

Elliot Are you sure that doesn't feel / right

Noah It's / right

Aaron Who invented these things

Tamara / Don't cheat

Aaron They're sort of bizarre when you think about them

Noah Right. Ready?

They are all tied together in a circle of Christmas crackers.

Maud I think I heard once a story about a rogue batch, about a man who went around putting actual explosives into crackers and families around the country were blown to pieces across their dinner tables limbs everywhere, fingers in the sprouts, knee caps floating in the gravy. Heads missing. Children burnt alive.

Or maybe that was a story like a horror story like a Roald Dahl or something.

(*Counting the crackers in.*) Three, two –

Noah Wait. What's the braucha for Christmas crackers?

The heater turns off.

Aaron *Baruch atah Adonai aloheinu Melech ha'olam asher kidshanu b'mitzvotav v-tzvanu l'hadlik ner shel* Christmas cracker.

Elliot Amen.

Tamara / Amen

Noah Amen

Maud . . . Amen

> *And,*
> > *BANG – the crackers are pulled.*
> > *Cracker chat ensues, some people put hats on.*

Aaron Okay come on

Noah Yes

Maud URGH I'm starving

Noah Fuck yeah

Aaron Feed me / baby

Noah Smells gorge

Elliot Is that . . . ? Oh yes I like those things.

> *They start serving themselves food, building huge big plates and making satisfied noises as they go.*
> *They each work at their own pace, a little of this, a little of that.*
> *And then they start eating.*
> *And as they do a silence descends on the room.*
> *We watch as they eat.*
> *Each of them going about it in their own way: gracefully, doggishly, shyly, shamefully. They are in their own separate worlds, enjoying their food, sating themselves.*
> *This takes however long it takes.*
> *At some point we might notice that Tamara is bothered by something. She tries eating. Stops.*

Noah (*the food*) Fuck

Aaron I mean COME ON.

A train thunders through the room.
It passes.

Is that the Northern Line?

Noah Uh-huh.

Aaron Fuck.
That must get unbelievably annoying.

Noah Weirdly you sort of / get used to it

Tamara You get used to it.

They eat some more.

Noah Could you pass the
Thanks.

Elliot This is good. This is good food.

Tamara Is it the place on the corner?

Noah No the

They eat some more.

Aaron Those are fucking hell those are urghhh

They eat some more.

Tamara Which place?

Noah By the roundabout.

Aaron Did anyone else notice how many foxes there are out there? Like an unusual amount of foxes. Maybe I've been away too long but it seemed extreme like a film set or something –
Pass those.

After some more time, the rhythm of their eating slows. One of them at first, and then another and then another.
  Until eventually the tide has turned and they are now fighting their fullness rather than their hunger.
  They carry on valiantly for a little longer.

Maud Oh my God.

Noah I think I'm going to shit and vomit at the same time

Aaron Keep going don't think about it too much

Noah I can't I literally can't.

Tamara The way you eat is actually disgusting

Noah I wish I could bore a hole in my side like those cows

Maud What?

Noah You know when those cows get so full of gas or something they like puncture a hole in their sides and then they deflate and then they can walk around again
(*To Tamara.*) What?

Tamara Can you not that's disguising.

Elliot I think I know those cows I think I know what you're talking about

Tamara Stop!

Some time goes past.

It's like you're incapable of sincerity

Noah What?

Tamara I wonder how you bear it Maud it's like he's incapable of sincerity

Noah Just because I'm not . . .
I am capable of sincerity

Aaron She's right you are very bad at sincerity

Noah Are you actually joking
I'm like famously good at sincerity

Maud Famously?

Elliot I think we should watch the King's Speech

Tamara Why would we watch the King's Speech

Noah The film or like the thing where he –

Elliot The update from the monarch

Noah It's this thing where he sort of wishes everyone merry Christmas

Tamara I know what the King's Speech is!

Noah And I don't think people actually do that

Elliot Oh they do

Tamara Do they Maud? Do people watch the King's Speech?

Maud Erm. I think so.

Tamara And you *were* smirking Noah I could see you were smirking. Famously good at sincerity what a prick.

Aaron I don't think he / was smirking

Noah I was not smirking

Maud I'm not sure if he was smirking exactly

Tamara It's like you're scared of being part of something

Noah I'm not scared of being part of anything

Tamara And it was a smirk / I know a smirk

Noah / Oh my God stop it with the smirking

Tamara When I see a smirk

Noah Go on show me a smirk

Tamara I'm not showing you a smirk you fucking freak

Noah That's because I wasn't FUCKING SMIRKING!

The door opens. A man in a big coat, Felix, pops his head round.

Felix Scuse me is this Gary's place?

Noah Next door

Felix I ordered the ket?

Noah / Next door!!!

Maud Next door!!!

Felix is gone.

Elliot What's ket?

Tamara / NOTHING

Aaron / Ha!

Maud / Well it's

Noah NOTHING
And I'm not scared of being part of anything

Tamara You know he bought that Christmas tree Aaron?

Aaron Did you actually?

Noah IT'S A FUCKING TREE WHY IS EVERYONE GETTING SO STRESSED ABOUT A FUCKING TREE.

A moment.

Sorry that was an overreaction.

Aaron This is becoming a very Jewish Christmas

Noah What the HELL does that even mean
Sorry I . . .
But no seriously.
What does that mean?

Aaron You know what it means it means –

Noah No tell me. Tell me what it means.

Aaron Like . . . argumentative or / I guess

Noah I know what it means what I'm saying is . . .

Aaron Is what?

Noah Nothing.

Aaron Articulate your boy isn't he Elliot?

Elliot Is this sushi? Is this what sushi is?

Maud Er. No. This is . . .

Tamara This is Chinese food Dad.

Elliot Mmmm. It's delicious.

A moment.

Maud So Aaron you've been in Tel Aviv is that right? Noah was saying that you've been –
How's it . . . How's that . . . Has it
How has it
Have you
How has that been.

Noah Have you heard the thing about the fire in the woods

Tamara What?

Noah I am capable of sincerity I resent that I've actually made a lot of progress in –

Elliot Have you ever been to New York Maud?

Maud Erm

Tamara What's that got to do with / anything

Noah New York what do you mean New York

Elliot Have you Maud? Have you visited?

Maud Errr
No.
No I haven't.
I went to Disneyland Paris.
Sorry that,
That kind of made sense in my head but now I say it out loud I –

Elliot It's amazing it's . . .
Wonderful place. New York.
Sorry Noah you were

Noah Sometimes I think it would be better if it was twelfth-century Spain and we were all just listening to Maimonides and eating barley.

A moment.

Tamara Are you okay?

Noah No.

A long moment.

I mean yeah obviously I'm fine I mean

A moment.
Eventually:

Here's some sincerity.
In a time of crisis a prophetic man would make his way into the woods.

Aaron Story time!

Noah It's early medieval it's the Middle Ages and we're in Iberia in Portugal maybe. There's a renewal like they feel close to the covenant I suppose to the –

Elliot The covenant? What the hell is all this / religious

Noah And when the people were in crisis the man who was closest to God, he would go into the woods and he would light a fire and he would meditate in prayer.
And when his meditation was done he would return to the people and their problem had been solved.
Do you know this?
A generation later the descendant of this prophetic man would do the same. But the problem was that this descendant didn't know the place where his ancestor had gone. That information had been lost over time.

The rumble of a train in the distance, which grows over the following. The Christmas lights flicker.

And so the grandson instead he just entered the woods and he didn't light the fire but he said the prayer and his people were saved. A generation later now and they had not only forgotten where the fire was lit but they had also forgotten the prayer and so they travelled to the woods and they said: Hashem we do not know where the fire was lit and we do not know the prayer but we know that there was a fire and we know that there was a prayer and we come here to remember those things and again the people's problem was solved.

And now. Many many generations later. And the people are in trouble once again. But they don't know where the fire was lit. They don't know the prayers. And they don't even know where the woods once were. All we know now is this story. And all we can do is tell it.

The train has passed.
A moment.

Tamara Yeah I mean sorry but what the hell was sincere about that?

Noah I don't know. But that is basically how I feel one hundred per cent of the time.
Like the grandchild of the grandchild of the grandchild of the grandchild of the grandchild of the grandchild of the grandchild of the grandchild of the grandchild of the grandchild of the grandchild
Of the grandchild
Of the grandchild
Of the grandchild
Of the grandchild
Of the . . .

Silence.

Maud So Aaron. You moved.

Aaron That's right

Maud And how's that been. I imagine it's been . . . Being in a new place being in a new country starting a new life and with everything . . . I've always wondered what it might be like to be able to move to a new place and –

Aaron Honestly? It's like being at the fire in the woods.

Wren Yo.

They all scream.
Unbeknownst to them, Wren has stumbled into the room. He wears pants and nothing else.

Tamara Wren what the –

Elliot JESUS

Aaron Who the fuck / are you

Maud WOW

Noah It's Wren
Are you okay?

Maud He lives here

Aaron Wren? You're called Wren?

Wren seems a little dazed. It's as if he doesn't quite know where he is, as if to him this world in front of him is not quite as real as the one he lives in.

Wren You called you've called? You've been calling?

Maud Erm . . .

Noah Huh

Maud I don't think so

Aaron What do you mean called what are you saying what is he saying

Tamara Is everything okay? Everything okay up there?

Wren Me fine yeah uh-huh yeah of course what it's just I thought you called? Like you called out and I'm plugged in you know

Aaron Does he always dress so well?

Tamara (*to Aaron*) Stop it

Maud Do you need help? Is everything okay

Wren Fuck off yeah

Elliot Excuse me

Noah Wow

Maud It's okay

Wren I just thought you called? I was sure that you you definitely called that's all I'm you know it isn't right it isn't right to call someone and then to turn like that to turn your back you know no I'm okay you're okay I like you I like you really I do like you okay we get it you're smarter than me okay okay big deal you're smarter sure university books blah blah blah and yeah you're good looking sure you're good looking uh-huh you're a good looking man but just fucking no no you're okay you're okay not on Christmas

Wren turns around to exit back the way he came. And as he does, he reveals a huge gash down his side. It's a fresh wound, the blood runs.

Maud / My God

Elliot Good / Lord

Maud Wren?

He spins back round suddenly, locks eyes with Maud.

I . . .
  I think you've . . .
  I think you've hurt yourself.

Noah Would you
Would you like something to eat?

Elliot Noah

Aaron Noah I think he –

Wren I'm going for a walk

Noah Okay sure

Wren It's Christmas Day isn't it. That's what I'd do. With my family. I'd go for a walk after Christmas dinner.

Wren strides across the room. From somewhere he takes a large overcoat. He throws it on. And walks out the front door, shoeless.

Maud Should we

Elliot You live with this man? You live under a roof with this man?

Noah He's fine I think he's probably actually fine

Aaron He didn't seem fine he looked like he was about to go shoot up a school

Tamara You were rude

Aaron I wasn't rude I was –

Tamara You were fucking rude

Aaron I didn't want him to bleed on me he told her to fuck off

Noah How did he even get that

Maud Should we –

Noah He's fine he'll be back he's fine

Elliot Ket. Ket means ketamine doesn't it.

Maud Did he even put shoes on

Noah I'm pretty sure that was Dexter's coat by the / way

Elliot I think I need to lie down is there somewhere I can lie down

Tamara You know I was thinking Aaron that story you told earlier?

Noah I don't think he had shoes on

Maud It's cold out there

Elliot I need to lie down

Tamara I'm sorry I just wanted to say that you sounded like a parody. Swimming naked in the Mediterranean with your mates you sounded like a parody account and I feel like we didn't rinse you as thoroughly as we should have

Maud Are we sure he's okay are we sure Wren is okay out there

Noah He does wander off sometimes / to be fair

Tamara (*a mock Euro-Hebrew voice*) Come to Tel Aviv baby eat falafel and find yourself an olive-skinned Israeli girl.

Aaron Oh I forgot I've got these mushroom drops? My friend grows them and makes them into this tincture thing they're actually gorgeous let me one sec does anyone want

Elliot No more food for me.

Tamara (*still in the voice*) The drugs are super fantastic and super clean there's like no comedown and dude you can chill in these crazy sick bars

Elliot I'd like to lie down for a while

Aaron You just need a couple they're actually extremely chill

Aaron pipettes a few of the drops onto the back of his hand and licks them off.

Tamara (*still in the voice*) It's like the Levant is pulsating through me with life and pussy and crazy fresh fruits

Noah (*joining with the same voice*) And the tech-house scene is crazy bro

Tamara Do you like tech-house bro?

Noah I literally live for tech-house. Have you been to Burning Man?

Tamara I basically started Burning Man my guy

Noah (*his own voice*) Wow I think I'm hungry again

Tamara Tel Aviv. It's the Berlin of the Middle East.

Aaron It actually is though

Snapping back to her normal voice like a shark:

Tamara Israel. Importing Germany's club and genocide culture since 1948.

Elliot slams his fists on the table.

Elliot Watch your fucking mouth

Noah Tamara!

Tamara What?

Aaron The fuck?!

Noah Can we not. Please. Please. Can we not. We've been doing so well.

Tamara Not what? Talk?

Noah That is not what this is

Elliot How dare you what the hell do you know

Tamara I thought you were going to lie down

Aaron You can't say that kind of thing it's so fucking –

Tamara What?

Aaron Offensive

Tamara Oh you're worried about being offensive now are you?

Aaron Fuck you

Noah Calm down Tam

Maud Is anybody going to check on / Wren

Tamara Fuck you I am calm he just told me to fuck off tell him to calm down

Aaron I didn't tell you to fuck off I said fuck you

Tamara Anyway it's how we talk it's fine it's normal.
　I hate it more than anything when you tell me to calm down Noah
　It's . . .

She grabs a Tupperware full of food and starts eating.

Aaron These beaches Maud. In Tel Aviv. I'm not talking Brighton or Skegness. I'm talking sand, I'm talking white beaches as far as the eye can see.

Tamara Truly white beaches if you know what I mean Maud

Aaron I . . .

　　　What . . .

　　　　　What does that

　　　That doesn't even . . .

Noah Can I have some of those drops?

Noah goes and gets the drops, squirts some on the back of his hand and licks them off.

Elliot What does it mean all this white stuff why are you always talking about this white stuff I don't understand what the hell you mean

Tamara Where's that rice thing?

She puts down the empty Tupperware, hunts for another. Finds one. Keeps eating.

Aaron I stand taller. Like I physically stand taller over there. That niggling thing, you know. In England. That not-quite-belonging thing

Tamara Have you looked at your phone?! Look at your phone. How can you say these things when all you need to do is look at your phone / and see

Aaron It's there don't try and deny that it's there

Tamara Yes you poor poor thing North-West London really treated you rough. You can walk around England with more sense of belonging than ninety per cent of people in this country

Aaron That's not true

Tamara It literally is

Elliot It's ours you know. You know that. It's as simple as that. It's ours.

Noah What

Elliot It's ours and stop wishing it away.

Tamara If you want to lie down Dad you can go to my / room

Elliot It's ours and that's that stop fucking you know with your talking and your . . . it's ours, okay?

Tamara What are you talking about

Maud I would actually watch the King's Speech but to be clear I never have watched it before

Elliot Is that what you want? Are you some kind of . . . You're sitting there minding your own business enjoying your day when some fucking Arab pops up from out of a tunnel and chops your head off. Is that what you want? How can't you see that

Tamara Stop it

Elliot It's just the truth Tamara I love you but that is the truth killing Jews that's what we're talking about

Noah How did this happen why are we doing this

Tamara (*to Elliot*) Why does that matter so much to you

Noah Tamara

Tamara No I want to know I want to know why you are so obsessed when one Jew dies. What is so special about a Jew dying? I don't get it. I don't get what is so much more special about Jews dying.

Elliot I hope you're not being serious

Tamara I'm being deadly serious

Elliot Don't make me answer that question.

A moment.

Noah Is there dessert?

Maud Yes that's a / good

Aaron Because it matters more when it's us.
Obviously.
Obviously it matters more when it's us.

A moment.
And then,
suddenly,
Tamara vomits.

Maud Tamara

Elliot Fucking hell

Noah Tam

Aaron Wow

Maud Let me . . .

Tamara It's fine it's a thing it happens calm down Jesus I'm fine.
I'M FINE I said
Carry on let's carry on.

A moment.

Aaron Do you want a mint I think I've got a . . .

She glares at him.

Sorry.

Eventually:

Elliot These are the facts my darling. This is how it is. This is the cold reality of things.
You know sometimes it's like you refuse to see the world as it is you're so unrealistic – it's ours. Sorry I don't mean it like that that sounds cruel but I hear you speak and scream like a . . . Well to be frank, my angel, I hear you scream like a child at a party like a child who's had too many sweets at a party and I think to myself how was I not able to get this into your head?
You know?
It's sweet really, it's idealistic I suppose but I mean grow up my darling. To be honest that's what I think I think grow up. It's ours, that's that it's just ours.
And then you throw a word like that around as if you know anything. Shouting isn't going to help darling you use a word like that, and I'm sorry I know you're upset clearly you are but you go around as if you know a single thing as if I didn't as if IT'S OURS OKAY and thank fuck for that IT'S OURS TAMARA they had their chance and they said no it's as if you know nothing about Oslo I mean COME ON we give them a shithole like Gaza and look what they do to it . . . If you had been there in my house with my mother with my . . . If you had seen it if you had watched the tanks roll in and if you had smelt her breath on a Tuesday morning with the blinds down . . . If you had

FUCK IT'S OURS NOW IT'S OURS OKAY IT'S OURS PLEASE JUST LET IT BE OURS please just allow that to be the case allow that to stay the truth I'm really sick of this shit I'm sick of this it's like it's happening again but this time it's YOU it's YOU and your mates your posh university mates your English mates without a fucking clue who they are or what it is or which way is up and which way is fucking down and it makes me feel like I've failed like I'm the broken link IT'S FUCKING OURS ALRIGHT

A moment.

Sorry.
   I'm sorry.

A moment.

I'm going to lie down.

Maud You can use / our

Noah Do you want me to show you –

Elliot NO
(*The mushrooms.*) What are those things?

Noah Nothing Dad don't worry they might send you a bit . . .

Elliot lies down on the floor.
The heater turns on. They watch it for a little while.

Noah I think we might have missed the King's Speech but we could watch something else like *Harry Potter* or *Die Hard* or that Jimmy Stewart film what's it called –

Aaron This diaspora you're so obsessed with Tamara. It's a trauma. You know that don't you? And you don't have to be here. This doesn't have to be your home

Tamara But it is. It is my home.

Aaron I think what I've realised is that this was never my home

Tamara You never gave it a chance

Noah *Life is Beautiful* is the name of the Jimmy Stewart thing I've never actually seen that

Maud Really?

Aaron This meal. This food. This isn't an English thing. This isn't a thing that English Jews do. Chinese food is what non-Jews think Jews do on Christmas. You're like a Jew minstrel. This Chinese food thing is an American thing and don't pretend that you don't feel disconnected from it. You're not Larry David, you're from Hendon. And you're grasping at straws for an identity.

Tamara Says the newly branded Hebronic Übermensch

Maud How do you I just don't understand how you come up with these words so quickly

Aaron Fucking hell you two celebrated Christmas I remember turkeys in your house

Tamara That is not what that was that was like one year

Noah It was most years Tamara

Tamara You shut up

Maud I'm pretty sure it's not called *Life is Beautiful*

Noah Really?

Maud *Life is Wonderful* maybe?

Tamara It's called *It's a Wonderful Life*.

Noah What's *Life is Beautiful* then

Tamara It's an Italian / holocaust film.

Aaron It's an Italian holocaust film –
  (*Straight back to it with Tamara.*) And you know all this diaspora stuff it wouldn't be so sad if there wasn't a more glorious option

Tamara Glorious? Fuck me Mr Smotrich

Aaron That's too simplistic.

Noah Does anyone else want some of these?

He squirts some drops directly into his mouth.

Aaron They were socialists Tamara actually doing something don't you want to be there for that?

Tamara Socialism? That's what socialism looks like? I refuse to believe that the choice we have is between murdering and being murdered

Noah Who's we?

Aaron / What?

Tamara What

Noah Who is this we you keep talking about

They look at him, confused.

Tamara In the beginning God filled everything

Aaron Oy

Tamara Listen.
In the beginning there was only God. He filled everything and there was only his glory.
And then he performed an act of self-limitation. He contracted in order to make way for creation. Do you understand?

Elliot That heater can we turn off that heater it's roasting

Maud I didn't know you believed / in God

Tamara It's a story. Listen.
He contracted. Because without contraction there can be no creation because everything is God. So we should see, then, the creation as a kind of exile. God removes himself from himself. He puts himself into exile. So as to make way for the created world.

So the experience of exile is an experience that God himself knows. It puts us so close to him.

Aaron The holocaust does not make me closer to God

Tamara I didn't say that

Maud Why is the heater staying on like that Noah

Tamara And it does, by the way.
Most people on this planet. For most of them life is fucking shit. Hunger. Death. Pain. For most people that is what life is.

Aaron It's crazy that you can say these things with a literal belly full of dumplings

Noah Jesus it's hot.

Noah goes to the heater. He fiddles with it. Trying to shut it off.

Tamara Listen to me.
The world that God created was not God. But it was created by him and so it was filled with his divinity. At the moment of creation all of his divinity finds its way into the material world but the material world because it is not God is not able to carry the weight of all that glory the vessel can't hold it

Elliot Turn that heater off

Noah I'm trying it normally doesn't stay on this long

Tamara And so at the moment the world was created, it blew up. The vessel smashed and everything was broken everything was shattered. It's I guess it's a kind of alternative? Like an alternative to Adam and Eve to Genesis some other creation story it's some Kabballah thing? And it says that in our world in the world that we have inherited there are only shards of the Almighty's divine light that's all there is these broken remnants of creation there is a great rupture in everything and the world we know is a desecrated thing because the moment of creation it was also a moment of destruction.

Noah starts hitting the heater.

Maud Noah stop that

He stops.

Noah We'll fry in here I'm starting to sweat

Tamara But there are shards of divinity everywhere. Maybe you see it in the veins of a leaf. Maybe in the eyes of the person opposite you on the Tube. Or a lover.
  Or maybe in the hidden beauty that exists in all things. But this kind of broken glory is everywhere. Don't you see it, Jack?
  Our history of exile is a glorious thing. The ruins of the diaspora are beautiful. Walk around a little. Stop trying to sweep them under the carpet.

Elliot stands up. He takes his top off. And lies back down.

Aaron It's a story Tamara you said so yourself

Tamara Of course it's a story I don't actually think it happened

Aaron And who made up that story?

Tamara Huh?

Aaron Some medieval peasant Jew in a swamp in fucking Western Russia whose kid has just been thrown down a well. This guy has a vested interest in coming up with a cosmology that confirms his rotten place in the world as divine.
  Things that are broken can be fixed

Tamara Not by building a nuclear armoury

Aaron It helps

Tamara You kill me when you say that

Aaron Because you have built your identity on pain. You have been telling yourself these stories for so long. Of suffering and shattering and Shoah and blah blah blah stories, I might add, that are just that, you have only met race hatred in history books Tamara don't try and claim otherwise

Tamara ME?! You're the one / who

Aaron FUCK ME it's hot in here –
   You have built your identity out of this stuff and so the prospect of improving things devastates you because you know that you will disappear when you realise that things can be absolutely fine.
   Don't give me this holy spirituality Tammy, you are holding your identity up like a battering ram, not a sacred flame

Noah I think I'm gunna die like I think this is actually going to make me perish

Tamara And how are you holding yours up then?

Aaron You're white you're fucking white

Tamara Oh thanks I hadn't realised

Aaron The way you talk you wouldn't know

Tamara You think I don't know that you think I don't –

Aaron You're just desperately trying not to be

Tamara And what's wrong with that? We weren't you know we weren't not until recently we weren't –

Aaron Because that's the whitest thing I've ever heard in all my life –

Tamara WE'RE THE BAD GUYS NOW I'M SICK OF BEING THE BAD GUYS I DON'T WANT TO BE THE BAD GUYS ANYMORE EVERYWHERE I LOOK IT'S BAD GUYS WE'RE THE BAD GUYS NOW.

   A moment.

Aaron Why is celebrating Christmas so horrifying to us

Tamara Because it's not ours

Aaron Exactly. Imagine Chanukah in Israel. You should all move.

Maud I might have some of those drops Noah

Tamara I want you to cry about the holocaust.

Maud Wow.

Elliot has his hands over his ears by this point.

Tamara Go on. I bet you never have.

Aaron Tammy.

Tamara No please. Do it. Come on. Cry about it. Really cry about it. Cry about Auschwitz. I promise it's not that bad. It feels good. You'll feel good.

Aaron You're not the devil Tamara. You are just in so much pain.

Noah You both sound like fucking algorithms!

A long moment. They all sit there in the growing heat. Eventually.

Do you think it's real.
   The covenant I mean.
   Do you think it was real.
   Do you think we were in touch with him do you think Moses was a real you know do you think he genuinely
   With God.
   Like do you think God is real
   I think that we had him.
   I think that we had him but I think that we have lost him and replaced him with you know
   Woody Allen or something.
   Tottenham.

Anxiety.
I think we bartered him away.
And for what for safety?
I think that's why I get a little kick every time something bad happens. You know if a deli gets shot up or someone posts something you know something so obvious this guy I know the other day he posted this picture it was like so clear it was these skeletons? And there was a guy with literal devil horns and a big fat nose it was so blatant and it made me giddy, it made me actually happy to see it this is a friend this is someone I like.

I think I like it and I think that's because it makes me feel in touch with the covenant. Does that make sense? I sort of miss the pogroms. Maybe that's what I'm trying to say but I'm too . . .

I fucking hate being Jew-y but then like yeah I really want to be very very Jew-y.

Yeah I think I miss the pogroms.

And maybe that's why we hate them you know maybe that's why we

We see their God you know

We see that faith

We see how eviscerated they are

How holy

And it reminds us of us

Of what we had

And it confronts us too, it confronts us with the emptiness we now feel

And so we hate them.

Yeah,

because

well

I've seen an X-ray of a child's head, and it shows a sniper's bullet in their brain.

So like, what do we do with that.

It's like

Killing us didn't work. But turning us into them did.

A moment.
Elliot stands up. Walks over to the heater. And beats the living shit out of it.
Eventually both he and it are done.
He comes and sits down at the table.
Although they are all stunned by the violence, they are relieved by the cool.
A long silence.

Elliot Could somebody pass me my shirt please.

Maud collects his shirt and hands it to him.

Thank you.

He puts it back on.
A moment.

Maud We could carry on with the quiz?

Noah / Sure

Tamara Yeah

Elliot / Fine

Aaron Uh-huh.

Maud Oh. No that was a joke. Obviously I was joking.

Aaron Come on ask a question.

Maud Really?

Noah / Yes

Tamara Yes come on

Maud Erm. Okay.
Don't be stupid obviously not.
Really?

She reads from her phone.

What's the world's longest river.

Aaron / The Nile?

Tamara The Nile

Noah / The Nile

Elliot I'm pretty sure that's the Nile.

Maud Yeap.
That's actually the last one so

Silence.

Tamara My therapist said that silence can be good. When you stop talking, like that's when stuff actually happens. You allow stuff to happen. Talking actually kind of stops things from happening.

Aaron Maybe stop talking then.

Silence.
  Then,
  All of a sudden,
  The front door opens.

Maud Oh thank God –
Oh.

Felix, the man from earlier, pokes his head round.

Felix Hey

Noah You?

Aaron Is that the ket guy?

Felix Sorry are you sure this isn't Gary's place?

Tamara You're still here how are you still here?

Felix Couldn't find Gary's place could I, got stuck in a stairwell kicked my way out.

Noah It's across the courtyard in the other building next door.

A moment.

Maud Shall I show you?

Felix That would be splendid.

Maud gets a coat and goes to the door.

Maud Come on.

Tamara Noah.

Noah What –

She nods after them: obviously.

Sorry yeah coming coming.

Noah follows them out.

Felix (*as they leave*) Do you know if he's still got some of that delicious M-Cat it seems we're in the midst of a drought doesn't it . . .

They're gone.
Tamara exhales. They sit there for a little while.

Aaron Is he . . . ?

He points at Elliot, who has fallen asleep.

Tamara He does that more and more now.

They watch him sleep for a little while.

He's getting older. Funny to watch it happen.

Aaron You're very hard on him

Tamara Stop it.

Some time.

What?
WHAT?

Aaron Nothing.

A moment.
 She starts laughing.
 And they are both laughing now.
 An exhale.

Tamara I mean. Come on. This is funny. This is funny that we're sitting here and it's like Christmas or whatever.

Aaron Tamara.

Tamara Uh-huh.

Aaron We should talk.

Tamara Urgh. No thanks.

Aaron Tam I . . .

Tamara (*an impression*) Tam I . . .
 You're okay mate.
 God that was fun wasn't it. I forgot how good a sparring partner you are. I can't fight with other people the way I can fight with you.

Aaron I think we genuinely scared your brother

Tamara We argue the same way we used to fuck did you notice that?

Aaron What

Tamara Do you ever think about that? The way we used to.

Aaron shrugs.

JackJack. Jacky-Jacky-JackJack.
 Shy boy huh?

Aaron No.

Tamara Yes.

Aaron You always made me feel . . .

Tamara What?

Aaron Like a

Tamara Like a . . . ?

Aaron Powerful. You made me feel very powerful.

Tamara Wow.

Aaron Shut up

A moment.

Tam I'm . . .

Tamara . . . You're what? Use your words man Jesus.

Aaron I guess I'm sorry

Tamara You guess you're sorry.

Aaron I'm sorry

Tamara Sorry for what.

Aaron For everything. For how it ended.
For my deficiencies in the communication department

Tamara No?? You?!

Aaron I wish I had been better

Tamara Oh stop it. I was very sick Jack. And I was no angel. It's okay.

This hits him. He fails to hold back a sob. She watches him.

It's nice to see, you know.
    You. Broken. I wish you'd shown me more of that.

She puts a hand on his cheek.

Let's put some music on. Wake him up.

Tamara turns,
   Aaron grabs her,
   Spins her around –

And kisses her.
They kiss.
And kiss.
Eventually, Aaron pulls away.

Aaron Sorry I . . .
We shouldn't –

Tamara Wow.

Aaron Sorry.

Tamara You taste the same.

Aaron Fuck.

Tamara starts laughing. She can't contain her happiness.

Sorry.

Tamara Stop saying sorry.

Aaron Uh-huh.
What?!

Tamara Nothing nothing I'm just . . .
I'm just very happy right now that's all. I feel like I'm in the right place.
Come here.

He does.

Hold me by the back of the neck.
Take your right hand. And hold me by the back of the neck.

Aaron He's going to wake up.

Tamara He won't.
Come on. Hold me by the back of the neck.

He does.

Squeeze.

He does.

That feels . . .
You have a kind of caveman in you don't you. I never told you this I was so angry I didn't . . . But when you fucked me it was like having this mute dumb caveman on top of me and it was fucking glorious.

They kiss.

Aaron You taste . . .

Tamara Mmm?

Aaron You taste a little bit of sick.

Tamara Oh my God!

Aaron Faintly

Tamara JACK

Aaron A whisper of vom

Tamara / No

Aaron It's just a hint like a suggestion

Tamara You're lying

Aaron Like a White Claw, but sick

Tamara SHUT UP.

Aaron To be completely honest I actually quite like it.

Tamara Disgusting boy.

A moment.

Is it too much to admit
    That when you held me like that, when you squeezed me
    I felt myself get a little bit wet
    I felt myself slip on myself.
    Does that make you feel powerful?
    You can stay here tonight. It's fun. It's a fun life we have.
    Really you should this place is wild in the morning there's
like twenty people here and you recognise half of them and

the majority are insane like I mean genuinely clinically unwell not just neuro-spicy like neuro-explosive you'd enjoy it

Unbeknownst to them Elliot has woken up. And he is watching them.

Hey.
   Look at me.
   Look at me I said.
   You're okay my darling boy.

She kisses him.

You're not fooling me. I see you. Stay with me tonight. I'll look after you.

They kiss. It escalates and eventually Aaron throws her down somewhere, Elliot still watching when –
The door opens and in come Maud and Noah.
Aaron moves away.

Maud / WOW

Noah Jesus

Maud Aaron!

Noah / What the fuck

Aaron Sorry –

Tamara Okay okay calm down whatever

Maud / What's going on Aaron

Noah That's crazy
   Dad?!

Elliot Huh?

Tamara / Sorry Jesus calm down you guys get with each other the whole time I literally never say anything.

Maud Aaron
   Aaron what are you doing? What are you doing Aaron?! What the hell are you doing??

Tamara Erm excuse me Maud.

Maud Aaron.

Noah Maud

Tamara What?

Maud Aaron.
Aaron come on.
This isn't right. This is just not right. Noah. Noah this isn't right.

Something's up.

Tamara What

Aaron Tam I'm sorry I

Tamara I know. And it's okay.

Aaron No I'm sorry I
I mean I'm . . .

Maud You're . . .
Noah for God's sake

Noah Not here

Tamara What do you mean not here / what's wrong

Maud Fuck I

Noah Fucking hell Maud

Maud Fuck I sorry I didn't mean to
fuck
oh fuck fuck fuck

Tamara Can someone please tell me what the fuck is going on?

Noah Jack. Do something.

Aaron Not here obviously not here

Tamara Are you sick?

Aaron We can go next door we can do this tomorrow

Tamara What's wrong are you okay? Is everything okay?

Elliot He's engaged, darling.

A moment.

Tamara Excuse me.

Elliot Your mother told me. We saw each other at shul last week she showed me a photo. Beautiful girl. Mazel Tov.
 You shouldn't be doing that kind of thing when you're engaged boychick.
 We won't be able to come I'm afraid it's El Al I just can't deal with El Al anymore. He's engaged. Aren't you.

Aaron I've been meaning to
 It's
 Yeah. We're getting married next year. In Haifa? She's a . . . Scorpio.

A moment.
 Tamara laughs.
 Stops.
 Laughs again.

Tamara You're . . .

                        what?

No you're not.
 No you're not.

Noah Why don't we go upstairs / we could

Tamara What are they talking about is this a joke?

Elliot I'm sorry my darling.

Maud Noah, Elliot, maybe we should go for a walk?

Noah Yeah sure that's –

Elliot You know sometimes I watch you Tamara it's like watching your mother.

80

Noah Dad

Elliot Did you say you'd been to New York Maud?

Maud Huh?

Elliot You're very beautiful aren't you

Noah What

Elliot If I were thirty years younger

Noah Oh my God –

Elliot I might not look it now but you know I could go. In my day –

Noah Jesus –

Elliot Young women break my heart into a million pieces you really do

Noah STOP

Tamara I really think I'm actually going to throw up again.

Maud Come on Noah, let's go for a walk. Elliot, we should go.

Elliot No this is good this is a good thing. Don't be sad. Don't be sad sweetheart. I think this is it, isn't it? I think this is what I've been . . . It's okay it's all okay . . . Yes, yes this is it because you know Sarah's pregnant.

Noah Huh?

Maud Who?

Noah What

Elliot Sarah. She's pregnant.

A moment.

Noah As in your girlfriend Sarah? She's what?

Elliot Pregnant

Noah Are you . . .
What
Wait you mean you're –
She's pregnant? You got her
And is she going to have an abortion?

Maud Noah

Noah You've known her six months what are you talking about

Elliot We're having a child.

Maud This is too much this is too much information in one go

Elliot I'm going to be a father.

Noah You already are a father

Tamara Am I dying?

Elliot I've sold the house and work have let me move to the US office. We're moving to New York. We're having a child and we're moving to New York. I find you all very inspiring.
You know Maud New York has always meant a very great deal to me.

Noah You've sold the house / as in

Elliot My mother left Europe in the middle of the century you'll be interested in this Maud

Noah Dad what are you saying we haven't / spoken

Elliot LET ME SPEAK. PLEASE LET ME SPEAK.
I can do what I want. I'm an adult and I can do what I want. And it's not too late it isn't too late I can throw someone onto a sofa and snog them too.

Noah (*that word*) Snog?

Maud Noah

Elliot I've been meaning to tell you. Sorry I haven't quite had the . . . It's harder for us. This stuff. It's like I haven't got the it's like I haven't been given the it's like I feel the . . . but I don't have the . . . You all you seem to have . . . I hope you understand that. I promise I'm trying. I promise you this is me trying.

My mother, Maud, arrived here by boat

Maud Yes Noah mentioned this –

Elliot Has he. Has he really. That's funny it's not something I –

Noah What is this we don't do this now we do not do this now

Elliot She left the mainland before the war.

They were taken on by some Polish humanitarian who got them to France and from there they boarded a ship to New York

Maud But I thought she was . . . Your mother? Noah I thought she was in the –

Noah / Not now

Maud And this was before the war?

Elliot And so she set sail across the Atlantic to the new world.

Noah Tamara I don't understand he's having a kid? How is he allowed to do that how are you just allowed to do that?

Elliot A few days later they found themselves pulling into harbour.

My mother stood there on the ship's deck waiting for the fog to clear. Any moment that famous statue would emerge and it would signify the start of her new life, the streets of New York.

And the fog did clear.

But no statue appeared.

Instead
she was greeted by some squat
white
cliffs.

And at the sorting office the men had strange accents and the food was wet and bland and everyone – she used to say – seemed hunched over from some kind of invisible force from above.

It wasn't until a month later that she discovered she was in England. Lincolnshire. And then Coventry. And then Manchester. I don't think she ever quite recovered from the shock. She had a kind of muteness deep inside her, my mother. Set there in terrible stone. Sometimes I think that it wasn't the Polish countryside that haunted her. It was England.

He looks up at them in a kind of ecstasy, with a kind of agonising joy:

We're going to start again. We're going to live in New York.

Silence.

Tamara I saw something
 I
 I saw it this morning
 It was a
 A cartoon posted by some guy some moron I know but it was
 It was kind of disgusting actually but in some ways like it was crass but also there was something
 It's a mother and her daughter huddled in a basement in a bombed-out building in Gaza.

There's rubble and bodies and bombs overhead and they're there the last two clinging on to life in this desolate wasteland. And up above their heads is a fighter pilot with his finger on a trigger ready to drop his final bomb on these final two people. And the daughter looks up to the pilot and she turns to her mother and she says: Mum. Why are we doing this to us?

I thought it was a typo.
Why are we doing this to us.
I dunno. Maybe it was.

Elliot What the fuck has that got to do with anything?

And then,
A kick on the front door.
Nobody moves.
Another kick. Decisive, commanding.
Maud stands, and slowly makes her way to the door.
She puts her hand on the handle.
She looks back at them.
Back at the door.
And opens it.
Wren is stood there.
He wears his overcoat.
His chest is smeared with blood,
And in his arms he holds the body of a dying fox.
He enters the room and slowly walks towards the table.
They watch him as he walks.
Standing above the table now he lowers the fox down to rest,
Holding the animal with a kind of care we might not have thought possible.

Wren I found him out there.
Out on the street.
He must have been mauled
His mother had left him
Though I guess she had her own troubles.
Poor thing.
Poor little wretched thing.

On the table,
The fox twitches.

III

It's later now. An end-of-the-evening stillness has descended on the space. Aaron sits somewhere.

Noah stands, holding a bin bag with something heavy in it. He looks down into it:

Noah Google says you have to call the council. They have this special collection service for dead animals? There're categories and apparently a fox is a medium. Small ones like rats and rabbits you just chuck in the bin but bigger things like foxes or dogs or mules – it said mules – for them you call the council and book a special pick-up.

I mean they're not going to do that until the New Year at least are they and I think it's already starting to smell? Can you smell it? It smells rotten it already smells . . .

That was fucking mental that whole thing was completely fucking mental.

I saw a thing on Reddit that said last Christmas a kid killed a duck in the park and wrapped it in wrapping paper and gave it to his grandma as a present. They just chucked it in the bin but they got a lot of hate in the replies.

I think you should probably leave to be honest man. Like before she comes back down you know. I don't think it'll be good if you're still here.

She hasn't been well. You do know that? I think you can probably see that. She hasn't been well and she's got this job which she fucking hates and she's all entangled in it and . . . I think today she was hoping that it would be a . . . I don't want her to have to . . .

You can leave your bag here I just really think you should . . .

Aaron I was gunna tell her

Noah Sure man I don't need to –

Aaron Really I was I just

Noah Totally yeah I get it I –

Aaron It's hard sometimes you know, saying stuff like that

Noah Sure.
Sure.
I mean.
Yeah I mean the issue wasn't really the not telling her you know the issue was the getting with her.

Aaron Right.

Aaron gets his coat from somewhere, prepares to leave.

I'm not a bad person.

Noah What?

Aaron I'm not a bad person.

Noah Oh I know that man you don't need to –

Aaron When I come back to England it's like I become a bad person again. It's like this place makes me feel like a bad person.

Noah I'm not saying you're a bad person man I'm just saying that by the time she comes down it's best if you're / gone

Aaron Life is much bigger over there you know.
It's intense but it's much bigger too and you don't have to worry about shit like
There's something epic about it. And then you come back here and it's . . .

As if the shitest thing ever:

Golders Hill.
I know a guy there he's from London he's called Dan? Dan Shea? You know him?

Noah shakes his head.

You probably do he was your year maybe year below. We've sort of become friends? He's sweet but he's not really the sort of person I'd hang out with normally you know he's like well to be frank he's a massive neek but he's nice and when you're in a new place you end up saying yes to things. Like you end up saying yes to getting a drink with a random person you wouldn't in London like a friend of a friend because you're trying to meet new people so the bar's kind of lower? It's weird but it's cool too. It's actually like a really healthy thing it takes you out of your comfort zone. It's been really good for me it's made me less judgemental, more open to the world more open to different people.

Noah Should I call an Uber?

Aaron Anyway me and Dan are mates now he lives around the corner from me in Tel Aviv and he's in the army?

He's normal. He's like very chill he's a normal guy. He smokes weed and makes his own pasta. And he's a reservist in the army. You know he's been fighting these last few years.

He told me this thing once when we were at mine. We were watching *Nathan for You* and we were pretty stoned and he was on a break between tours and he told me that you can hear the crunch. When you roll over a skull you can feel the crunch vibrate up through you from inside the tank. There's a popping like you're going over a football. He's a tank guy in the army you know when they go into . . . whatever.

He said at first he didn't know what it was. Then he realised and it made him feel weird. But eventually he just accepted it. Like a branch or something that goes snap.

He went back in the next week but apparently it was much more AI stuff that time and he actually works from a few neighbourhoods across so it's not as bad.

Anyway he told me all this and then we played this game we always play where we try and flick gummy bears into this lampshade I've got in my flat that's kind of like a bucket.

You know this is a normal guy this is just some Jew from Bushey this is just some guy my sister went on tour with.

Noah And how does that make you feel?

Aaron Huh?

Noah You know. How does that make you feel.

Aaron Oh.
Erm.
I guess. Sort of. Like. Neutral? That's how it is isn't it. That's what it's like. The world you know. I mean I'd rather it was him than me but I suppose I feel grateful. I suppose I feel a sense of gratitude?

God I feel sick maybe that food was bad have you ordered from that place before do you feel sick?

Noah You've got IBS Aaron you've always had IBS

Aaron (*pointing at himself*) Jew.

Noah (*smiling*) Yeah.

Aaron (*the fox*) Starting to go rank that thing. You should just chuck it out. Put it in the neighbour's bin or something.

Maud enters, followed by Tamara.

Maud He's having a shower Noah he's much calmer now –

She sees Aaron and stops.

Aaron Hey. Yeah.
Tam Tam.
Tam-alam-alamlam.
Right. Okay. Got my coat.
Uber's outside so I'm / gunna

Noah Maybe you / can

Aaron Yeah.
I'll call maybe?
Alright.
(*A mockney accent.*) Happy Christmas!

He leaves.
A long moment.

Noah We should clear up a little. Gabz'll be back soon.

Noah starts clearing up the space. Tamara and Maud stand there. Eventually:

Tamara You know he's not Jewish.

Noah Who isn't.

Tamara Jack. He isn't Jewish. Not really. Well. I shouldn't say that but, yeah. He isn't really not like us.

Noah It's been a long day Tam shall / we

Tamara His dad is like a quarter or an eighth something? And his mum converted, not even formally, he was brought up like us but he's not Jewish Jewish you know not really.

Noah I'm sorry what?

Tamara Yeah.

Noah Jack?

Tamara Aaron yes.
He told me at Boomtown in like 2013. We were on the ground outside a tent. I suppose he was feeling vulnerable.

Noah His mum? But she's like . . . She's like SO JEWISH.

Tamara Funny isn't it.

Noah She's like, Anne Frank Jewish. She's the Jew-iest thing I've ever met.

Tamara Yeah she's like some Protestant from Lewisham.

Noah That makes absolutely no sense. She's like the dictionary definition of Jew, she like . . . makes ME feel antisemitic.

Maud Noah.

Noah Wow.

Elliot enters. He is freshly showered and seems transformed. Put together. A well-polished front.

Elliot Righto then folks.

Noah Dad –

Maud Elliot how are you

Noah Are you feeling okay?

Elliot Fine. Totally fine.
For a shithole that's not a bad shower. What's CeraVe? Absolutely covered myself in the stuff.
Right I'm off. Thank you all for . . .
What do you say at the end of Christmas Maud? Thank you for a lovely . . . ?

Maud Erm. Christmas?

Elliot Thank you all for a lovely Christmas.

Tamara Do you want company?

Elliot No, no I'll be fine

Noah How are you gunna get back you're not getting the Tube are you?

Elliot Train doesn't run on Christmas boychick. I drove.

Tamara You can stay here if you'd like there's lots of spare beds

Elliot No, no.

Noah The Tube isn't running did you say?

Tamara You really can stay it's not an issue –

Noah If the Tube isn't running, then what's that sound?

Elliot's at the door now.

Tamara Dad.

Elliot Uh-huh.

Tamara Can I come with?

Elliot What's that.

Tamara Can I come with you.

Elliot Come with me?

Tamara Yes.
Can I
Can I come home?

Elliot looks at her. Nods.
Tamara takes a coat, goes to him.

Elliot It's just repairs Noah. They run repairs on Christmas Day so some of the Tubes still go back and forth. That's what that sound is. It's just repairs.
Come on now.

Maud I'll lock it behind you.

Elliot and Tamara leave. Maud follows.
Noah sits there.
He looks around. Tries to distract himself.
Eventually he moves over to the bin bag. He opens it, and looks down into it.
He gives it a big, deep sniff.
He puts his hand down into the bag. Prods around a little.
He lifts his hand up and takes a look at his finger.
He puts his hand back in and lifts it up, blood on his fingers now. He inspects it.

He puts his hand back in and out – covered now in blood and innards.
He puts his head in his hand.
And remains there for a little while.
Suddenly, shocked, he wipes his hand down his shirt,
His arms,
His other hand.
Somehow,
He's covered now in blood and guts.
Maud enters.
She looks at him and –
A short sharp scream.
And silence now as they look at one another.
The moment passes and Maud rushes over to the sink.
She finds a bucket and fills it with water, collects tea towels and comes over to Noah.
She wets a tea towel and goes to clean him when –
He lifts a hand to stop her
and she relents.
They sit there together.
Eventually:

Noah I used to think dread was one of those fleeting emotions. You know like a camera flash or something.

But my chest is like . . .

Maybe for a whole year now.

One thing I've learnt is that dread can stay with you for a very very long time.

Maud Let me –

He flinches away from her.

Did you . . .

Your grandma. Was she . . .

Like was she in the holocaust or

It's just you've always said that she was in the holocaust but your dad said that . . .

Noah Imagine if it didn't happen.

Maud That's what I'm asking you Noah

Noah No I mean imagine if the whole thing didn't happen. Do you ever think about that? Like maybe it didn't happen.

Maud The holocaust?

Noah Yeah.

Maud What do you mean?

Noah I dunno. Everything else has fallen to pieces. Maybe it didn't even happen.

Maud The holocaust.

Noah Uh-huh.

Maud Yeah. I mean I'm pretty sure it happened

Noah Uh-huh. But imagine if it didn't.

A moment.

Maud Come on let me –

She goes to clean his face but –
He shakes his head.

Stand up come on let me clean you it's not right it's not healthy.

Noah I'm fine I'll have a shower

Maud Come on

Maud tries to get him to stand up.

Noah What are you doing –

Maud Come on get up

Noah Maud stop it
What the fuck are you –

That tickles
Stop STOP
Maud

They are tussling now.

(*He shouts now.*) GET OFF ME STOP IT FUCKING STOP IT MAUD.

They break apart. Look at each other.

What the fuck is wrong with you Jesus.

Maud I want to clean you. I want to clean you on my hands and knees. I want to clean you like a newborn child.

He laughs. It doesn't quite work.

Sometimes I can't tell if you think I'm a freak in a good way or a bad way.
    You're terrified of me aren't you.

Noah I'm not terrified of you.

Maud Then let me in.

Noah I'm genuinely so tired

Maud YOU'RE NOT STOP LYING YOU FUCKING LIAR DON'T YOU KNOW I CAN SEE WHEN YOU LIE LIKE THAT THE WAY YOU AVOID ME THE WAY YOU RUN IT MAKES ME WANT TO PLUCK OUT YOUR EYEBALLS AND GRIND THEM INTO DUST AND SCATTER THEM INTO THE FUCKING SEA I'VE GOT A WORLD INSIDE ME TOO YOU KNOW THAT DON'T YOU I'VE GOT A WORLD INSIDE ME TOO.

A moment.

This fucking Jew stuff, I'm sick of it!
    That's not what I . . .

A moment.

Come here.

He comes to her.

Take this off, it . . .

She takes off his shirt. She takes it over to the bin and throws it away.

My mum died at Christmas you do know that don't you.

She was a Quaker. I think anyway I can't really remember she was an unstable person she'd . . .

At Christmas time she'd put her hands on our heads and she'd pray. She'd evoke Christ. She'd bless us in his name it was this strange thing she did.

It was just me there in hospital when she was dying. The nurse told me it was time and that I should hold her hand so she knew that she had company.

Take off your trousers

Noah What

Maud Off.

He takes off his trousers.

Even before she was sick she was damaged she had these outbursts she was a violent mother she'd hit us she'd whisper these terrible things in our ears she'd push her thumbs into our . . .

She picks up his trousers, takes them to the bin.

I was so angry with her I . . .

I looked down at her hands and all I could see were these weapons.

There was a café like a shitty café in the hospital with a bleak little Christmas tree. I got a hot chocolate and went on MSN Messenger. I talked to some random guy from school about fingering it was weird.

Half an hour later the nurse came down and told me she was gone. And then I just sort of went home.

She gestures to him with a nod.

Noah Maud

Maud Do it.

Noah Why I don't –

Maud Please.

He takes off his socks. He takes off his pants.

Good boy.

*He is standing naked now in the light of the tree.
She looks at him. And smiles.*

It's like you've been knocking on your own door my darling. No wonder nobody's been answering.

*She takes the cloth and dips it in the water.
And she begins to clean him. Squeezing the bloody water back into the bucket.
By now, Noah is weeping.
Once she has finished, she goes and takes a blanket from somewhere and wraps it around him.
She holds him.*

Noah When I forget, you know

When I forget that I'm Jewish. That I'm English that I'm a man, that I'm white, that my name is Noah and my sister is Tamara and my feet are here on the ground and I am –

When I forget all that

When I'm able to forget I get this kind of transcendent feeling. The dread lifts. I get this kind of transcendent lightness. And I love you but in a way that doesn't hurt so much. Like I'm walking into something infinite. Like I'm borderless. I become porous with the world, we breathe with the universe we get this kind of . . .

    This

                This sort of

This

                        Yes.

Yes that's it.

                        It's a kind of –

And then,
   Keys in the front door.
   It swings open brashly.
   And in marches Gabz.

Gabz OI-OI!!

She is dressed head-to-toe in a very elaborate Christmas elf costume. She's very merrily drunk.

What have we here? Coupla cunts!
   Fuck me up the arse I'm drunk.

Maud Gabz

Gabz Merry Christmas one and all. Like fox city out there you been outside?

She offers her cheek to Noah.

Gis a kiss then you fit fuck.
   Wait.
   Actually wait.
   Maud. Do I have your permission?

Maud smiles.

Maud Well that depends.

Gabz Depends on what.

Maud That depends on whether you've been naughty or nice.

Gabz Very nice, very nice indeed. I've done the cleaning rota twice and I've been using the toilet brush after I do a shit just like you taught me remember?

Maud Well in that case you have my permission.

Gabz Go on then.

*She offers her cheek to Noah
    Who goes to kiss it,
    And at the last moment she turns so he kisses her on the mouth.*

OH FUCK ME what a Christmas treat!

She does a little 'Christmas treat' dance.

Right. You don't mind if this merry little festive slag puts on a few Chrimbo bangboys do you? Another couple of hours until the world is shit again.

Gabz links her phone to a portable speaker somewhere. This takes a while. She dances to herself as she fiddles.

Why do these things always take so . . .
    Disconnect your fucking mum! How does it not even . . .
    There we go. Now we're cooking. Now we're bloody cooking.

She scrolls, looking for a song to play.

My Spotify Wrapped is literally all the Crazy Frog I've honestly no idea how it happened I played it at one party once I think the algorithm is set up against me.
    Right what have we here what have we here . . .
    BANG. That's it. That's my boy.
    Could it have been anything else?

*She presses play.
    'Lonely This Christmas' by Mud starts playing through the speaker.*

Alright dumplings. I'm going to clean. Does anybody mind if I clean? My uncle gave me a line of gear before I left – he's a fucking merchant – I'm feeling sharp I wanna clean is it alright if I clean?

Gabz gets a broom from somewhere and starts sweeping the room.

Fucking hell. I'm pissed as a Christmas rat.

You could light me up like a Christmas pud.

I think I had six bottles of wine. And two pints. Or no. Two bottles of pints and six wines? There was Baileys at some point. There was definitely Baileys. Baileys is fucking glorious innit. Better than coming, I reckon. I think next year I'm going to drink it year-round. Me in the pub in July. A pint of Baileys please barkeep. On the rocks. Straight up.

Wow.

Yeah I'm definitely drunk.

Jesus.

Drunk as a skunk. Pissed as a rat. Smashed as a . . .

Yeah.

Hardly know who the hell I am.

The music plays as a train moves through the space.
Gabz cleans.
For a moment, they all look so small in this vast space.
And then:
Blackout.
The Christmas lights flicker.
End.

Acknowledgements

Very many people made this play possible.

Thank you to the extraordinary National Theatre Studio, home whilst I wrote *Christmas Day*. I am particularly grateful to Nina Steiger and Sasha Milavic Davies for their faith. To Jeanie O'Hare, Ed Madden, Ola Animashawun and Stewart Pringle. And to Chrissy Angus, Temisan Nunu, Izzy Carney, Rachel Twigg, Jane Suffling, Miles Cruden Smith, Natasha Wright, Katy De Main and Sarah Clarke.

To Georgia Green, an early believer.

To everyone at the Almeida, and to Rupert and Steph in particular for their immense support.

To the sublime James Macdonald.

To Nigel, Samuel, Callie, Bel, Jamie, Jacob and Jessica for your bravery.

To Sophia Golan, compassionate sage.

To Miriam Buether.

To Liv and Maris.

To Lily, Jodi and Dinah at Faber.

To Rachie, for everything.

And to all our mothers.